TALKING IT THROUGH

No more bullying!

Rosemary Stones

Illustrated by Pat Ludlow

Happy Cat Books

When I was in the Infants I liked going to school.
My teacher was called Mrs Hughes. She was nice.
My best friend was Amanda Wood and I also played
with Ricky, Jason, Tracy and Samantha.

But when I was in the Juniors I didn't like school any more.
My new teacher, Miss Jackson, was all right
but a girl called Lisa Austin began picking on me.
That was the start of the bullying.

Lisa always had lots of new clothes
and shiny shoes with straps.
The other girls would stand round her and say,
"You look fab, Lisa!" "Can I try your shoes on?"
"I wish my hair was like yours."

Lisa said I had ugly, clumsy shoes and
only boys wore t-shirts like mine.
The others started making fun of me too.

"Lanky locks!" "Big feet and dirty old shoes!"
"Is that your dad's t-shirt?"

I asked my mum if I could have shoes
like Lisa's but she said no. They weren't practical
for school and besides, they were too expensive.
I was cross with mum for not letting me have
the right shoes, although I knew she couldn't
afford them.

The next day at school when it was playtime
Lisa told everyone not to play with me.
She said I had nits and I smelt.

Everyone started holding their noses
and running away from me.
Amanda didn't hold her nose but she didn't
come and play with me. She was afraid of Lisa.

That night my gran came to stay
and she gave me a present.
It was a pencil case shaped like a banana.
Inside there were pencils, a pen,
a pencil sharpener
and a rubber
shaped like an apple.

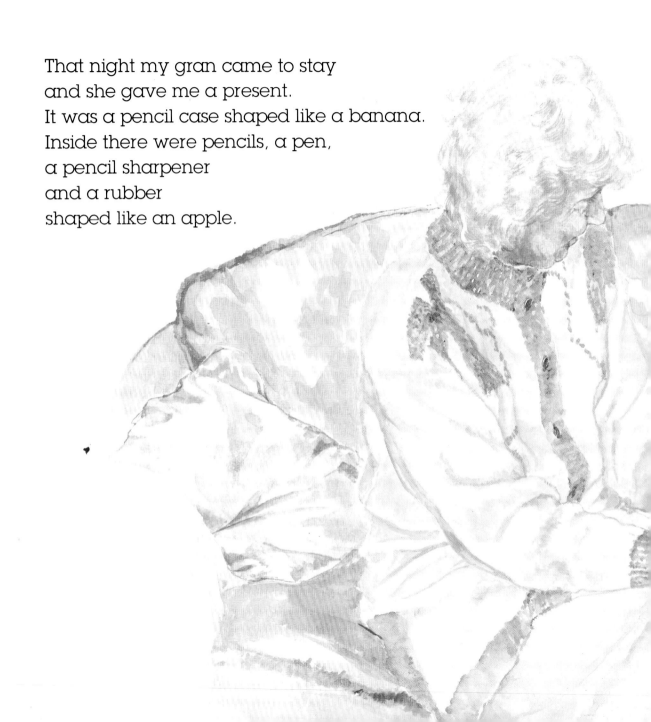

I told Gran I'd take it to school next day to do my work.
I was pleased I had something new that was so nice.

Miss said my pencil case was lovely.
I wrote about it in my news book and drew a picture.

Then it was wet playtime
and we all had to stay in and read comics
while Miss had her coffee in the staffroom.

Suddenly, Lisa grabbed my pencil case
and wouldn't give it back.
She undid the zip and tipped everything out.
When I tried to get it back, she threw it to Ricky
and he threw it to Mark. Everyone began throwing it
round the classroom over my head, even Amanda.

I thought I was going to cry.
I could feel my face going red.

I grabbed back one of my pencils just as Miss came in.
"What are you up to, Anna?" she said in a cross voice,
"Go and sit down quietly." She wouldn't let me explain.

I got all my things back but one pencil
was broken and the rubber was all dirty.

The next morning I told Mum I was ill
but she said I was just being lazy.
I had to get up and go to school.

I wanted to stay out of Lisa's way so when
Miss asked for a volunteer to tidy the book corner
at playtime, I stuck my hand straight up.
Miss chose me but Lisa leaned over
and whispered, "We'll get you later, Smelly."

At home time I asked Miss if I could clean the blackboard
but she said, "Off you go and stop dawdling."
Lisa and Ricky jumped out at me by the gate
and grabbed my lunch box. I ran after them
and found it on the pavement.
The thermos flask was broken.

Mum was cross about the thermos flask.
I said I'd dropped it.
I was afraid she might come into school
and complain about Lisa and Ricky.
Then I would get it worse.
Lisa would set everyone onto me.

At the weekend, Mum and me went to the market.
I saw Lisa and her big brother out shopping.
"That girl goes to my school," I said to Mum,
"and I wish she was dead."
"What an awful thing to say, Anna!" Mum said,
"Don't let me ever hear you say that again about someone."

Mum didn't ask me
why I didn't like Lisa.
I thought then there was
no one who could help me.

On Monday two big boys from the comprehensive
came to our class. Miss said they were going
to be helpers so that they could learn about us.
They were called Ronnie and Paul.

At breaktime Paul and me told Miss about the bullying.
I felt terrible at first, a real telltale.
But Miss was nice. She believed what I said.
I told her about the pencil case and the thermos flask
and no one playing with me and the names and everything.

"It happened when I was in top Juniors," said Paul.
"A boy stole my dinner money. I told Mum I'd lost it.
Then he said he wanted more money and his gang
would get me if I didn't give him some.
I took money from my mum's purse
because I was so scared of him.
Mum found out the money had gone
so I had to tell her about the bullying.
She helped stop it."

"I can't tell," I said. "It'll be worse if I tell.
Besides, Miss won't believe me."
"I'll help you," said Paul.

At reading time Paul talked to me.
"Why are Lisa and the others nasty to you?" he asked.
"They're only messing about," I said, "it's nothing."
"It's not nothing," said Paul, "it's bullying
and I know what that's like. I used to be bullied.
It made me hate going to school."
I was so surprised.
I didn't think anyone
could have bullied Paul.

When Miss wasn't looking
Lisa pushed my chair away
so that I fell over and banged myself
and Ricky threw my news book across the room.
I didn't know that Paul was watching them.

When I'd finished, Miss said, "I'm glad you've told me
and I'm sorry I didn't realise what was going on.
You're not a telltale, Anna. You're a sensible girl
who wants bullying to stop. And so do I.
I'll have a word with Lisa and the others."

The next day Miss told everyone
there was a surprise in the hall.
The teachers were going to act a play for us.
It was such a funny play. Miss acted a girl bully
who hit everyone and called them names
and frightened them.
Sir acted a boy who was being bullied.

Then there was a big discussion about bullies
and what Sir should have done not to be bullied
and why Miss was a bully.
Everyone put their hand up to say something.
Sunita said if she was bullied she would tell,
it wasn't being a telltale.
Amanda said perhaps bullies were people
who were bullied by someone else.
Ricky said he thought bullies were afraid
and so they pretended to be hard.
Wendy said that bullies should be punished.
Jason said you should feel sorry for them.

Sir said we would have lots more talks about bullying
but did anyone think bullying was a nice thing to do?
Everyone shouted out "No!"

Then it was playtime.
I felt nervous but it was nice.
Amanda asked me to play two-ball
and then we played skipping with the others.

Lisa is all right now although she's not really my friend.
We still discuss bullying with Miss from time to time.
I'm glad I told and there's no more bullying.